# The Christmas Santa Had
The Sniffles

To Julia & Nicholas & Thomas
And Christmas every year
I love you!

Coppyright@2020 Gail G Wood

All rights reserved.

Live Like T Publishing

Houston, Texas

ISBN 978-1-7358114-3-7 (paperback)

ISBN 978-1-7358114-4-4 (ebook)

Santa stood by the big green board
Where the letters from all the good little girls
& boys were saved. He smiled at his busy elves.

Some were side by side, sawing and hammering and sewing up toys.
Others sat in a circle, painting and calling for colors.

By the Christmas tree, the elves worked in pairs. One called from a list and made a big red check as his partner gathered each toy.

Santa reached for a letter, but he stopped.
He sniffled.

He sniffled and sniffled again.
The elves dropped their work and turned to look at him.
And then....

The elves glanced around with worried looks.
And then something happened.....
The elves hammering and sawing sniffled.
The elves painting sniffled.
The elves checking toys sniffled.

Soon, everyone was sniffling and sneezing!

Mrs. Clause came around the corner. She took one look and said, "Oh dear," and bustled them off to bed.

Santa and the elves sniffled
and sneezed
and felt hot
and cold
and thirsty - all at once.

After everyone was settled, Mrs. Claus returned to Santa and asked,
"What will we do? Who will make the toys?
And who will deliver them to the girls and boys?"

She leaned over to hear Santa whisper,
"You must ask my friends to help."
"Of course," she nodded. "They will save the day!"

Chief Leprechaun heard a call on the wind. "Mrs. Claus," he called back, "we'll be there immediately!"

The friends arrived at the North Pole. They hugged and said, "Hello!"

They peeked into the empty workroom,
nodded to each other,
and knew just what to do.

The leprechauns chattered together
as they marched over and started hammering and sawing.
The bunnies hopped in and settled down to paint, smiling and whispering

The fairies flitted off calling to one another in their high voices and checking the toys off the lists.

Finally, the sleigh was loaded with toys and the reindeer were ready to go.

Chief Leprechaun and Mr. Easter Bunny clambered in as
Miss Tooth Fairy fluttered nearby,
then they flew off together into the sky.

Chief Leprechaun, Mr. Easter Bunny, and Miss Tooth Fairy laughed and sang and took turns going down chimneys.

When all the toys were delivered, they returned to the North Pole.
"Santa, we're finished," proclaimed Chief Leprechaun.
"The work is all done," whispered Mr. Easter Bunny.
"The girls and boys will be so happy," sang Miss Tooth Fairy.

Santa smiled and said, "Thank you, good friends. I could not have done it alone. You have saved the day!"

So, on Christmas Eve,
if you hear marching, or hopping, or fluttering of wings,

There is a very good chance that
Santa has the sniffles, and his friends are saving the day!

Made in the USA
Coppell, TX
19 November 2020